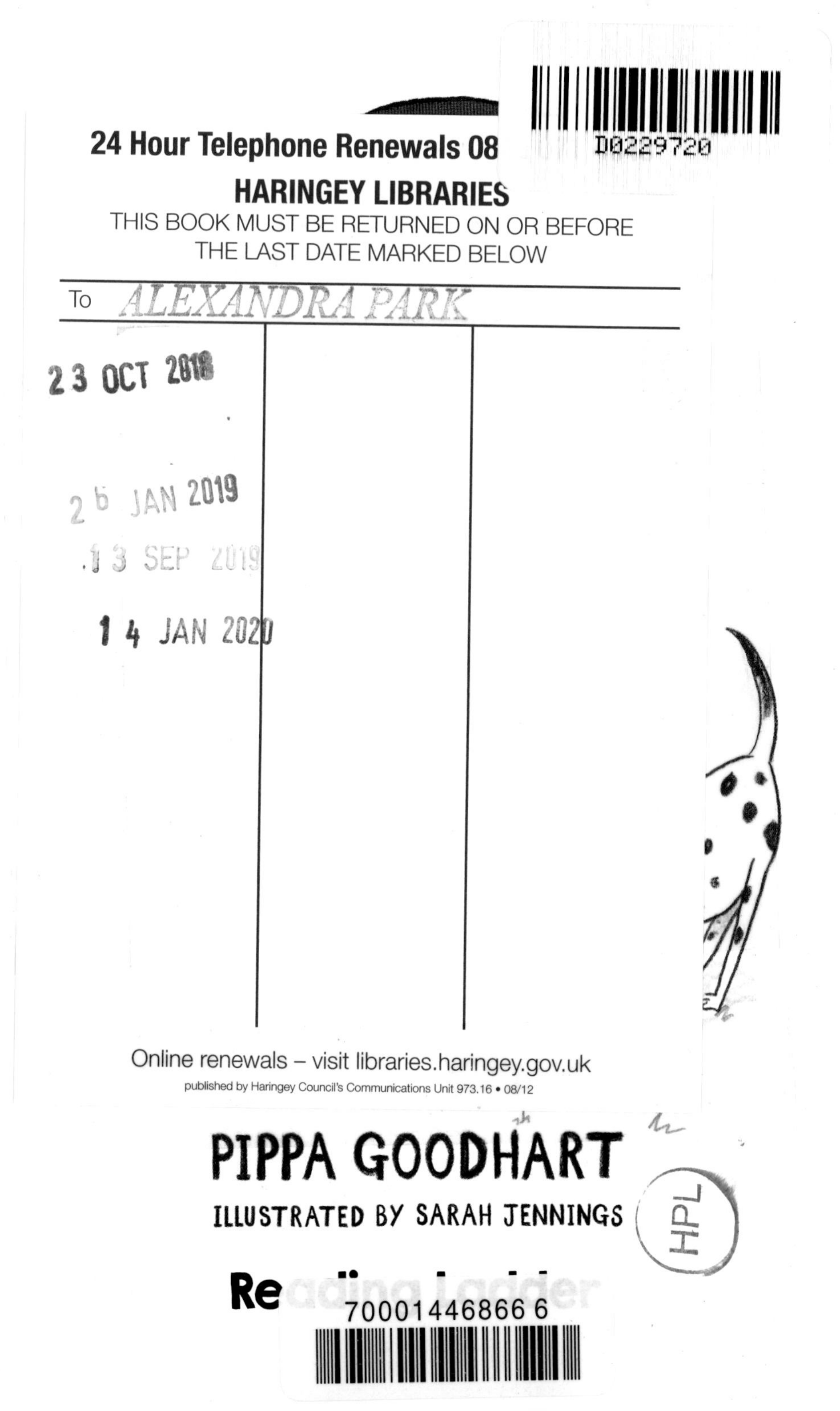

PIPPA GOODHART

ILLUSTRATED BY SARAH JENNINGS

Re

EGMONT

We bring stories to life

Book Band: Blue

Lexile® measure: 300L

This Reading Ladder edition published 2018
by Egmont UK Limited
The Yellow Building, 1 Nicholas Road, London W11 4AN

ISBN 978 1 4052 8643 5
www.egmont.co.uk
A CIP catalogue record for this title is available from the British Library.
Printed in Singapore
65669/1

Series consultant: Nikki Gamble

Chapters!

PG: For Paddywack, Elsie and Winnie,
my own three waggy tails

SJ: For Adie, thank you
for your endless support
and encouragement

Up, Up and Away!

Dots and Scruff were tall dogs.

Duster was a short dog.

‘Sniff sniff! What is that smell?’

Off ran Scruff and Dots.

‘Wait for me!’ said Duster.

‘Look at those flowers!’ said Scruff.

‘All I can see is wall,’ said Duster.

‘Wow, look at that food!’ said Dots.

‘Oh, I wish I was tall,’ said Duster.

So Dots and Scruff made a plan.

Dots tied a red balloon to Duster.

'Oh dear,' said Duster.

'Up you go!' said Scruff.

Only one end of Duster went up.

‘All I can see is wall still!’

said Duster.

‘You need a balloon at both ends,’

said Scruff.

She tied on a blue balloon.

Up went Duster.

'Now I can see the flowers and food,'

said Duster. 'I feel tall!'

But Duster went on going up and

up and up.

'Oh, no!' said Duster.

The wind blew Duster up and away.

'Duster!' said Scruff.

Scruff and Dots ran.

'Wait for us, Duster!' said Dots.

'I can't!' said Duster.

Jump!
Squeeze!
Swim!

POP!

‘Help!’ said Duster.

‘Got you!’ said Scruff.

‘Thank you,’ said Duster.

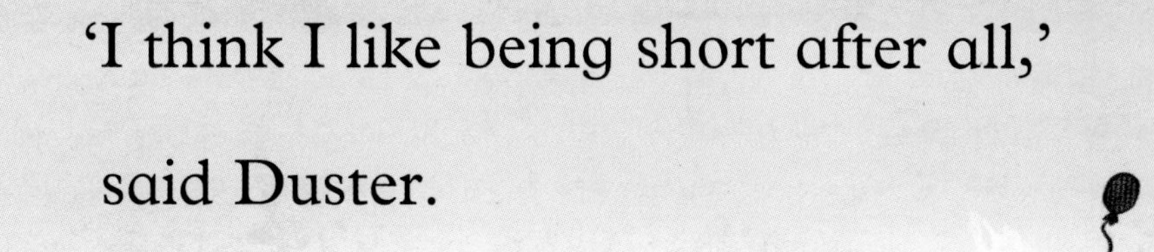

'I think I like being short after all,'

said Duster.

Lost and Found

Lost and Found

'Let's go out and find things!'

said Dots.

'Ruff!' agreed Scruff.

'Yap!' agreed Duster.

Scruff ran off fast.

'Wait for me,' said Duster.

'Hurry up, Dots.'

Sniff! went Dots.

Scruff ran on.

'Wait for me!' said Duster.

'Hurry up, Dots,' said Scruff.

'Hello!' said Dots to a squirrel.

Scruff ran round and round.

'You are making me dizzy, Scruff!' said Duster.

Off ran Scruff again.

'Wait, Scruff!' said Duster.

'Dots, do keep up!'

‘It’s getting dark,’ said Duster.

‘We need to go home.’

‘This way,’ said Scruff,

and she set off.

'Come back, Scruff!'

said Dots. 'Home

isn't that way.'

'Oh dear,' said Duster.

'We are lost!'

'It all looks the

same,'said Scruff.

'No it doesn't,'

said Dots.

'Look for

flowers like this one.'

‘Here they are!’ said Duster.

‘Good,’ said Dots.

‘Now listen for a splish-splash.’

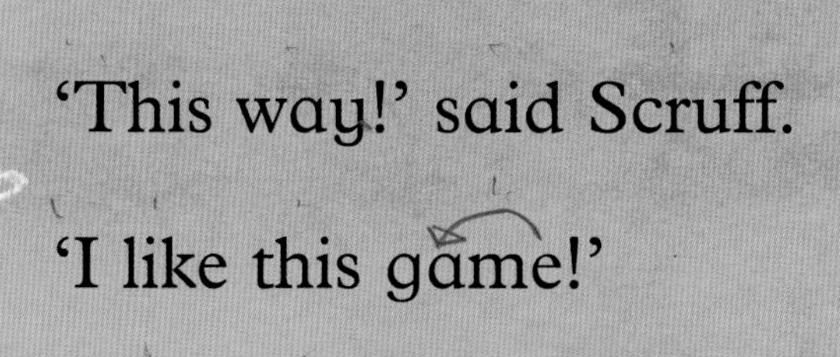

'This way!' said Scruff.

'I like this game!'

'Now look for leaves like

green dog ears,' said Dots.

'Here!' said Scruff.

'Now sniff for something pongy!' said Dots.

Sniff sniff

‘This lamppost smells!’ said Duster.

‘And there is home,’ said Dots.

‘*Ruff!*’ said Scruff.

They made a map of their walk.

'Next time I will stop and look at things,' said Scruff.

'And sniff and listen too,' said Duster.

'Well done, Dots.'

Surprise!

'We have a surprise for you, Scruff,'

said Duster.

'Hooray!' said Scruff. 'What is it?

What is it? What is it?'

‘It starts with you going away,’

said Duster.

‘Goodbye, Scruff.’

That was not a nice surprise,

thought Scruff sadly.

She was so cross that she dug dug

dug the ground and found . . .

'Wow! What a big bone!' said Scruff.

She felt a bit better.

‘But Dots and Duster would like the bone too,’ thought Scruff. ‘I know, I will give them a nice surprise!’

Scruff dug the bone.

Then she pulled and pulled.

'It is too big for me to pull out!'

she said.

So *chew chew*, Scruff made the bone a bit smaller.

Scruff took the bone in her mouth,

and set off home.

'This will be a nice surprise for Dots

and Duster!'

Clonk!

'The bone is still too big!'

said Scruff.

Chew chew!

Scruff ate a bit more bone.

And a bit more. And even more.

Oh dear!

Now the bone was very small.

'It isn't big enough for a nice surprise any more,' said Scruff.

So, *chew scoff*, she ate it all.

And she went home.

'Surprise!'

'We are having a party!' said Dots.

‘Oh!’ said Scruff.

‘That is a nice surprise!

You are nice friends! *Ruff!*’

'Just a very small bone for me,

please,' said Scruff.

And that was a surprise to Dots

and Duster!